CANNON THE LIBRARIAN

MIKE THALER

Illustrated by Jared Lee

AN AVON  CAMELOT BOOK

For
all who love books
and those special people
who tend them

AVON BOOKS
A division of
The Hearst Corporation
1350 Avenue of the Americas
New York, New York 10019

Text copyright © 1993 by Mike Thaler
Illustrations copyright © 1993 by Jared D. Lee Studio, Inc.
Published by arrangement with the author
Library of Congress Catalog Card Number: 93-90122
ISBN: 0-380-76964-6
RL: 2.0

First Avon Camelot Printing: August 1993

CAMELOT TRADEMARK REG. U.S. PAT. OFF. AND IN OTHER COUNTRIES, MARCA REGISTRADA, HECHO EN U.S.A.

Printed in the U.S.A.

BAN 10 9 8 7 6 5 4 3 2 1

Every day after school
I walk to our local library.

Miss Cannon is the librarian.
She is *very* special.

One day I was quietly reading about dragons...

when one swirled out of the book!

It towered over me, smoke curling from its nostrils.
I shouted for help!

Miss Cannon took off her glasses,
grabbed her ruler,
jumped over the checkout desk,

and pointed to the "No Smoking" sign.

The dragon snorted flames that burned up Biographies A through M.

Miss Cannon got mad,
grabbed a fire extinguisher,
and covered the dragon with foam.

The dragon burped,
and disappeared in a puff of smoke.

Miss Cannon jumped back
over the checkout desk,
put on her glasses,
and went back to stamping library cards.

Another day I was reading
a book about pirates,
and three of them sprang out!
They started singing pirate songs.

Miss Cannon said "Shush."
The pirates started switching
the drawers of the card catalog.

Miss Cannon got angry.
She took off her glasses,
grabbed her ruler,
and vaulted over the checkout desk.

The pirates growled
and waved their cutlasses.
But with one swing of her mighty
12-inch ruler, Miss Cannon sent them
scampering back into the book.

Then she waved her ruler wildly
in the air, cartwheeled
over the checkout desk,
and went back to mending worn-out covers.

Eight pages later, a giant octopus
slithered out of my book
and started tap-dancing on her desk.

Miss Cannon gave a little sigh,
tied his arms in knots,
and used him for a cushion
in the children's room.

Then there was the time
I was reading about Dracula.
He slinked out of the book and
was about to sink his fangs in my neck

when Miss Cannon tapped him on the cape
and pointed to the
"No Eating in the Library" sign.

He was so embarrassed
he turned red and sat down.
She gave him a library card
and a vegetarian cookbook.

Then there was the day she made the witch
sweep up all the frogs,

**and the trolls take the spell
off the drinking fountain,**

and the Martian pay a fine
on a travel book
that was 2,000 years overdue.
The fine was *very* big.

Miss Cannon has also saved me from Frankenstein,

dinosaurs,

and numerous ghosts, ghouls, goblins, and giants!

Miss Cannon saves me a lot.
She also lets me use her hanky
when my nose runs.

I love Miss Cannon.
In fact, besides the books,
she's why I go to the library...
every day after school.

Avon Camelot Presents Fantabulous Fun from Mike Thaler, America's "Riddle King"

CREAM OF CREATURE FROM THE SCHOOL CAFETERIA
89862-4 $2.99 US/$3.50 Can

A HIPPOPOTAMUS ATE THE TEACHER
78048-8 $2.95 US/$3.50 Can

THERE'S A HIPPOPOTAMUS UNDER MY BED
40238-6 $2.95 US/$3.50 Can

Coming Soon

CANNON THE LIBRARIAN
76964-6 $3.50 US/$4.50 Can